Gordon's Stroll

A Legend Old, a Poem Retold: Indian Leap

Gerard C. O'Brien

Natalie Schloesser, Illustrator

PAGE PUBLISHING
Conneaut Lake, PA

First originally published by Page Publishing 2022

Story Illustrations copyright Natalie Schloesser, 2022

ISBN 978-1-6624-7014-1 (pbk)
ISBN 978-1-6624-7016-5 (hc)
ISBN 978-1-6624-7015-8 (digital)

Printed in the United States of America

To the Great High Spirit who embraces us all

Acknowledgments

To my wife, Eva, for filling the gaps of my computer shortcomings.

To my daughter, Erin, and son, Jed, for their resurrected illustrations.

To my family's enduring patience.

To Natalie's persistent diligence.

Gordon M. Fisk's 1844 original sixty-three-stanza poem, "Indian Leap or the Great Cove," may be read at *Ludlow: A Century and a Centennial, History of the Town* by Alfred Noon, June 17, 1874, pp. 20–26.

Author's Note

Honorable Gordon M. Fisk was a poet, politician, and a publisher from Ludlow and Palmer, Massachusetts. He knew about "Indian Orchard" because early European settlers discovered plum orchards by the Chicopee River near Ludlow and Springfield. They had to be the "Indian's orchards" for no one else lived there before, people said. And so perhaps the life of the name began.

In 1846, Charles McClallan constructed the stone dam on the Chicopee River for the Indian Orchard Canal Company and found stumps of an old plum orchard while drawing down water for the canal.[1]

Yet Gordon wondered if the Indian Leap legend was true. Indian Orchard has its own Indian Leap Street off Main Street, and the Indian Leap House Hotel stood on Main Street until 1938. Retreating Agawam Indians fleeing Springfield's burning during King Philip's war in 1675 ended up at the Chicopee River in Indian Orchard and Ludlow by the Great Cove.[2] Yet only legend survived about an Indian's Leap.

---

[1] "The Village of Indian Orchard… History and Legend…" by Mary A. Blais, January 1976.

[2] "King Philip's War," George Ellis and John Morris, Grafton Press, 1906. Mass. records and archives, p. 119. Pynchon returns to Springfield, and Agawam Indians retreat to Indian Orchard, Chicopee River.

Moonlight lit the village as Gordon closed the door behind him. Embracing the frigid autumn air, he began his walk, whistling softly as he strolled along.

Soon emerged a familiar path, which he took. Winding between trees, he ambled along and found himself overlooking the Chicopee (Chicuepe) River.

Gordon looked down to see a small island breaking the deep calm waters. Soon, his eyes beheld a deep precipice, its red sandstone base at Wallamanumps Falls.

5

Suddenly, he heard hushed voices and watched spirits rise from the river. Gordon shivered. Upstream, the loud foaming falls failed to shut out these whispers that hinted of tragic bygone days.

Moving cautiously, Gordon stumbled upon another long narrow path. Down, down he went along the dangerous route then rested against an old white pine tree on a ledge.

Where did those Indians go? he thought, peering into the rippling water.

Gordon sensed these low voices were of the dead. He jumped up, lifting his voice loudly. "Tell me, sad river and silent rocks, where is that native tribe now?"

But only his voice echoed from across the water.

The river then became aglow as Gordon held his breath. Before him, an Indian appeared in a bark canoe. The brave paddled his craft toward Gordon, whose heart drummed with fear.

Stepping upon land in one stride, the young man drew his canoe ashore. Crouched down, this native son edged closer to Gordon as if on a vengeful mission.

The bold warrior stood erect as a statue, with his plumes and deerskins all tattered. His sheaf was empty of knife and his bow unstrung. The brave's stony chin pivoted heavenward as light sparkled from his eyes.

Eventually, Gordon spoke up. "Tell me, please, where are you from? What is your name? Have all your people gone?"

Slowly, the brave turned toward Gordon, fixing his eyes upon him. "Young man," the Indian answered. "It's you that brought me to this rocky shore where many times I walked before. I am immortal, and Wa-ha-waugh is my name. I come from the land of spirits, dressed as I did before."

Gordon replied quickly, "At first, I feared you. Yet now, I trust you bring me no harm, so answer, if you will. I've heard a legend about this cove, so tell me if it's true."

Wa-ha-waugh turned again to Gordon with fiery eyes. "The Great High Spirit sent me, for he knew you longed for truth. Deer roamed here as we hunted freely.

This peaceful land was our home. The Great Cove here gave us duck and fish aplenty. Our canoes glided over a calm river with never an enemy. Then over many moons, this changed as our comfort soured to war.

"Over the ocean, few settlers came as we shared our venison with them. In time, their number grew as a mighty nation they became.

Settlers cleared our forest and killed our game. They robbed our streams and treated us unfairly with broken promises.

"We saw their wrongs and set revenge within our hearts, barring our knives, stringing our bows, and filling our quivers. We burned their houses late at night and scalped young men who dared to fight. Some men we tied to a tree then decided their destiny.

15

"Our council fires burned bright at night as our victims moaned in atonement for their crimes. But more settlers became such a force. They slayed our braves right in our fields. We yielded the land around our streams, and here died the remains of my tribe."

The chief began to describe. "This is what happened.
"On the isle there below, our braves sat in council deciding the fate of two captives. As I declared their sentence, a band of settlers ready for battle rushed down the hill, startling us all.

17

"Our frightened braves paddled furiously to shore to confront them, but their hot muskets blazed, collapsing us from our canoes into the river.

On land, they pushed us hard toward the treacherous cove.

"We were trapped, and saw our doom with no path to escape. The steep cliff was before us, our enemies behind, and the spirit of death upon us.

"Surrender in shame or leap below was our choice. Clutching my young son, I ran to the cliff's edge and cried out to my warriors, 'Come, and be brave also!' In anguish, I leaped to my horrid death below. Valiant warriors followed me into their gushing watery graves as our sunken bones began their slumber.

20

"Gordon, do you still ask where my race is? Why my unstrung bow and empty sheaf? We died defenseless. It's been so long since your settlers took up our space. Greediness took us from our native place.

21

"Now, towering steeples rise next to your dwellings, replacing our peaceful wigwams—the ones lined with furs and stored with food, where children frolicked about. Go now, truthful one, go and tell thy kin of wrongs they've done. Farewell, my tale is done, for the Great High Spirit calls me home, and I must return."

Wa-ha-waugh, that forlorn chief, vanished before Gordon's eyes.

Gazing around, alone again, Gordon Fisk had a story to tell. He turned and strolled homeward, and upon reaching his front door, the town bell chimed the midnight hour.

23

Home now, Gordon found his bed and settled in, but sadness churned him from within.

Sleep wrestled his thoughts and slowly won, for he soon forgot the Indian Leap.

Glossary

Caughmanyput tribe. A legendary local tribe in the Indian Orchard and Ludlow vicinity.

Chicuepee. A Native American term for Chicopee, meaning, "rushing or raging waters."

Great High Spirit. The supreme spirit or deity worshipped by certain Native American tribes.

King Philip. Metacom or Metacomet, chief of the Wampanoag people. Second son of Massasoit. English nickname.

Legend. A story from the past that many people have believed associated with some people or nation often containing some facts but sometimes wholly untrue.

Roaring Thunder. Purported chief of the Caughmanyput tribe.

Wallamanumps Falls. "Redstone" falls and cliffs of Indian Orchard and Ludlow.

Indian Leap

(By the ninth-grade girls of Myrtle Street Junior High School, class of 1945; Indian Orchard, Massachusetts)

Near the Falls of Wallamanumps,
Near the haunts of Roaring
    Thunder,
Were the clean and tidy wigwams
The stout and worthy wigwams
Of the peaceful Caughmanyputs.
Near these Falls of Wallamanumps
On the Chicopee—clear and
    sparkling
Was the Red Man's encampment
On a point was this encampment
Where there glowed the Red Man's
    campfires.
Here they sat in peaceful silence,
Here they slept by the nearby
    waters,
The soothing, singing waters,
The roaring, tumbling waters,
The Falls of the Chicopee.
Here were found the Red Man's
    weapons,

Chips of flint and arrowheads,
Here they made their coats of
    bearskin,
Feathered dress and sturdy footwear,
Strung their beads and wampum
    shells.
A small tribe were these Indians,
These peaceful, friendly Indians
No war waged, they with Paleface
Or with Indians of the valleys
Or with Indians of the highlands
Or with Philip and his warriors.
Many legends have been told us
Of the sly and cunning Philip,
Of the Chief of Pokanoket,
How he organized the Red Men,
How he traveled far and wide.
Down the long and mighty river
Planning war against the Paleface.
Suddenly, with warriors many,

Came this chief—with speed and
    silence,
Came with fire and bows and
    arrows.
Soon the settlement blazed with
    fury,
Soon the stock and crops were
    ruined,
Leaving only death and sorrow.
Long ere sunlight lit the heavens
Came the White man, armed and
    ready,
Came with powder and with
    musket.
Searched they high and low for
    Philip,
For the sly and cunning Philip,
Who had burned the White man's
    village.
Searched the highlands and the
    valleys,

But in vain they searched the highlands
And in vain they scoured the valleys.
Suddenly, above the river
High above the swirling waters
Came they upon the peaceful Redskins,
The friendly Caughmanyputs.
Trapped were they, those friendly Indians;
One by one they turned their faces

One by one they leaped, and, diving,
Struck the jagged rocks and water.
Stalwart braves were they, and daring,
Fearless of the White Man's coming.
Then there stepped forth Roaring Thunder,
Clasping in his arms his offspring;
Backward sadly one look casting,
Leaping forward, fiercely yelling—

Down they fell, and all was over
Lost amidst the swirling waters.
Lost were they, those peaceful tribesmen,
And today we hold in memory
The place of their courageous daring,
The place of their fearless passing—
Indian Leap is what we call it.

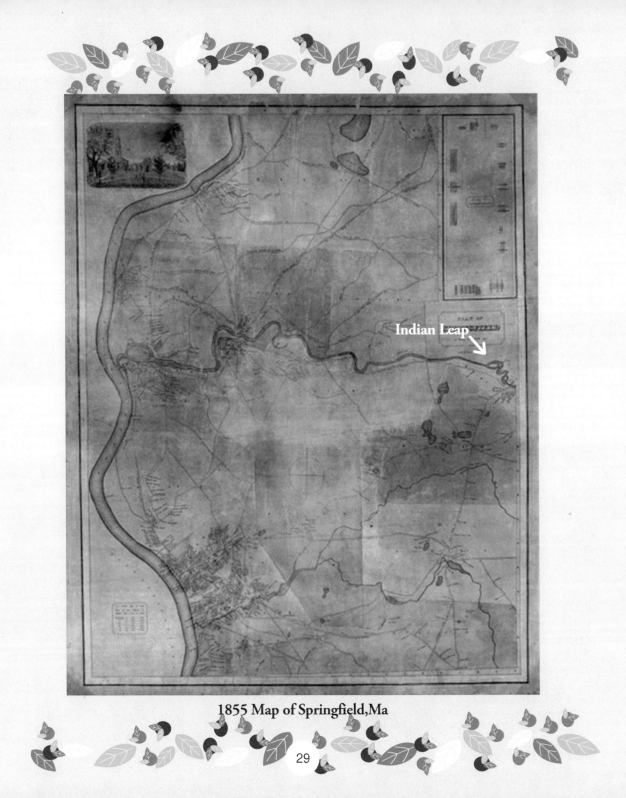

Indian Leap

1855 Map of Springfield,Ma

About the Illustrator

Natalie Schloesser lives in Ludlow, Massachusetts with her husband Norm. They have one son, Nikolaus.

About the Author

A retired schoolteacher, Gerard C. O'Brien has penned two children's books with illustrator Natalie Schloesser.

He resides in Indian Orchard, Massachusetts, with his wife, Eva. His four children and eight grandchildren keep him relatively busy.